The Striped Elephant

Be unique…be different

Anita V. Sanders

Content:

Chapter 1
The extraordinary birth

In the heart of the African savanna, where the sun shines brightly and life vibrates in every corner, an extraordinary elephant was born.

He was no ordinary elephant, but one who defied expectations and broke norms. This small being, which barely opened its eyes to the world, was covered in black and white stripes as if a zebra had lent it its fur.

The uproar did not wait. The herd of elephants, stunned and perplexed, watched the newborn. Guttural sounds of surprise and murmurs of confusion filled the air. They had never seen anything like it. Mother elephants lifted their calves with their trunks so they could observe the peculiar striped elephant. The oldest of the pack, with their time-weathered fangs, spoke in low voices, trying to find an explanation for this unprecedented event.

Meanwhile, the mother of the striped elephant, with eyes full of love and tenderness, protected him with her enormous trunk. Despite the shock that her son caused, she saw him as a perfect, unique, and special being. She named him Stripes, a name that reflected his unique coat and that would undoubtedly mark his destiny.

News of the striped elephant's birth spread quickly throughout Africa. Animals of all species came curiously to see him. Some mocked him, others looked at him with suspicion, but some admired him for his peculiar beauty.

Little Rayas, oblivious to the reactions he provoked, grew healthy and strong. His black and white stripes became a symbol of his particularity. As he explored the world around him, he learned to function in an environment that did not always understand him.

Rayas's birth was not only an extraordinary event in the savannah, but it also marked the beginning of a story full of adventures, lessons, and values that would lead him to discover his true place in the world.

Chapter 2

The search for identity

Rayas, the elephant with horizontal and vertical lines, grew up with insatiable curiosity. She looked at the other elephants, with their uniform gray skin, and wondered why he was different. Why did he have those boring tattoos? What did it mean to be a striped elephant?

One day, Rayas decided to look for answers. He headed to the wisest part of the savannah, where dwelt an old baobab tree, known for its ancestral knowledge.

"Grandpa Baobab," Stripes asked shyly, "why am I different from other elephants?"

The tree, in its deep, resonant voice, responded, "Stripes, the difference is not a curse, but a blessing. Your stripes make you unique and special. You are a gift to the savanna."

Grandfather Baobab's words filled Rayas's heart with hope. However, he still had many questions. What place did he occupy in the pack? How could they accept him being so different?

Determined to find his place, Rayas embarked on a journey through the African steppes. On his way, he encountered animals of all species. Some accepted him and celebrated him for his uniqueness, while others rejected him for being different.

One day, Rayas encountered a group of zebras. Seeing his stripes, the zebras welcomed him with joy. "You are one of us," they told him. "You're a zebra."

Rayas felt happy for the first time in a long time. At last, he had found a place where he fit in. However, something inside him told him that it wasn't quite right. It wasn't a zebra, it was an elephant.

A wise lion, observing Stripes' confusion, approached him and said: "You don't have to fit into a mold. You are a unique being, with your characteristics and abilities. Your place in the world is to accept yourself and be." yourself".

The lion's words resonated deeply with Rayas. Finally, he understood that he didn't need to be like everyone else to be happy. His worth did not depend on the acceptance of others but on his acceptance.

From that moment on, Rayas was filled with confidence and security. He decided to return to the elephant herd, not to be like them, but to share their uniqueness and teach them the value of difference.

Upon returning, Rayas was greeted with surprise by the pack. However, this time, the surprise was not because of his stripes, but because of the confidence that emanated from his being. When someone laughed at him, Rayas took it with humor, showing that those words did not hurt him, but rather showed how rude the other was. Rayas spoke to them about his experiences and taught them that diversity is a wealth that should be celebrated; that we are all different in some way or another, that we all have different strengths and abilities, and at the same time, that we are all weak in other aspects, hence the importance of helping each other and not making fun of each other.

Over time, Rayas became a respected leader of the pack. His story inspired others to accept themselves and value differences. The savanna became a more tolerant and harmonious place thanks to the legacy of the striped elephant.

Moral: The search for identity is a personal journey that leads us to discover our true value. Being different is not a disadvantage, but an opportunity to shine with your light. Accepting ourselves and celebrating our differences allows us to build a more diverse and harmonious world.

Chapter 3
The value of the difference

Rayas' return to the elephant herd marked a before and after. His striped fur, once a source of ridicule and suspicion, became a symbol of acceptance and respect; although many still doubted. Rayas, with his wisdom and experience, became an ambassador of the value of difference.

One day, while the adult elephants were drinking around a body of water, Rayas and the smaller elephants were on the top of a hill. This time the striped elephant told them a story.

"In a faraway land, there was a garden full of flowers. All the flowers were the same, with the same shape, color, and scent. One day, a different little flower sprouted in the garden. It was a multicolored flower, with a unique shape and a intoxicating aroma. The other flowers, seeing it so different, rejected it and ridiculed it. The little flower, sad and alone, began to wither.

A hummingbird, observing the scene, landed on the flower and said: 'Don't wither little flower. Your difference is your beauty. The garden needs your color, your aroma, and your shape to be complete.'

The hummingbird's words encouraged the little flower. Little by little, the other flowers began to see her with different eyes. They realized that their difference was not a defect, but a richness that completed the garden. From that day on, the little flower was admired and celebrated for its uniqueness."

At the end of the story, Stripes looks at the other little elephants and says: "Each of us is like a flower in the garden of life. We are all different, in our characteristics and abilities. And it is that difference that makes us special and unique. The pack needs diversity to be strong and thrive. We must learn to accept and value each other, not only for our similarities but also for our differences."

But... while Rayas was talking, and the adult elephants were still drinking water at a distance, a pride of hungry lions was slowly heading toward the baby elephants. Rayas warned him and told the little ones to run towards the adults. The lions saw these defenseless creatures running in front of them, but when they realized that there was a solitary zebra in the distance, they preferred to run after it. The closer they got, they realized that the zebra was bigger than they thought, and when they were just meters away from hunting it, they realized that it was not a zebra but "Rayas," the largest elephant in the savannah. Rayas used his long, sharp fangs to throw each lion that crossed his path into the air, making them all flee.

This dantesque scene resonated deeply in the hearts of the other elephants. They began to understand that difference was not a threat, but a blessing that had saved their offspring. From that day on, the pack became a more tolerant and harmonious place, where differences were appreciated and celebrated.

Moral: Difference is not a weakness, but a strength. Accepting and celebrating diversity allows us to build a richer, more vibrant world full of possibilities.

Chapter 4

Friendship without borders

The fame of Rayas, the tattooed elephant, spread throughout Africa. Animals of all species came to him to hear his stories and learn about the value of difference. Among them, a little rhinoceros named Rino became his best friend.

Rino was a shy and reserved animal. Unlike the other rhinos, he did not roar ferociously nor did he like to play fight. He preferred to read books under the shade of a tree or listen to Rayas' stories.

One day, while Rhino and Rayas were talking under a starry sky, Rino told him: "I feel different from other rhinos. I don't like roaring or fighting. I feel more comfortable reading and telling stories."

Rayas, with his understanding look, replied: "Friend, difference is not a bad thing. It is what makes you unique and special. You don't need to be like others to be happy. Be yourself and don't be afraid to show your true self." nature."

Stripes' words encouraged Rino. He began to accept his nature and let go of the expectations of others. He realized that he could be a strong and brave rhinoceros in his way, without needing to roar or fight.

The friendship between Rayas and Rino strengthened over time. They supported each other and celebrated their differences. Together, they explored the savannah, learned new things, and defended the value of friendship without borders.

One day, while walking in the meadow, they encountered a group of hyenas who were making fun of Rino for having reading glasses. "You're not a real rhino, you have four eyes, not two," they told him. "You are a weak and cowardly rhinoceros."

Rino, feeling vulnerable, looked to Stripes for support. Rayas, with his firm and confident voice, addressed the hyenas and said: "Rhino is a rhinoceros as strong and brave as any other. His difference does not define him, but rather makes him unique. True strength lies in acceptance and respect for others, regardless of differences."

While the hyenas were doubting what they heard, one of them was preparing to eat an orange grass that was growing between some rocks, but when Rino noticed it, he shouted "Stop! That grass is poisonous!" The oldest hyena approached and verified what Rino said, realizing that it was true. It turns out that this small bush was only born every 100 years, and that knowledge about its dangers was transmitted from father to son, from generation to generation, over the years. The old hyena asked Rino how she knew about those characteristics, and he answered that through a book.

Stripes' words resonated with the hyenas, who felt embarrassed by their behavior. They apologized to Rino, learned about his power of knowledge through reading books, and promised not to make fun of him again.

Rino, with Stripes' help, had learned to stand up for himself and not let the opinions of others define him. His friendship became a symbol of unity and acceptance, regardless of differences in race, species, or character.

Moral: Friendship knows no boundaries. True friends accept and support each other, regardless of differences. Friendship allows us to grow, learn, and be better people.

Chapter 5
The importance
of acceptance

The striped elephant had come a long way in his search for identity. He had learned that all beings have differences and that is why it makes them unique; But there are many who, without reason, judge the deferences of others as ugly and therefore believe they have the right to mock them. Rayas felt that he still needed to understand something more.

One day, while he was walking in the meadow, she met a wise old owl. The owl, with his penetrating eyes, saw

Stripes' internal struggle and said to him:

"Stripes, I see that you have learned to accept others, but you have not yet accepted yourself. Your zebra stripes are not a curse, but a blessing. They make you unique and special. You must learn to love and celebrate them."

The owl's words resonated in Stripes' heart. He realized that he was right. He could not love others if he did not love himself. He began to observe his stripes and discover the beauty they contained. He saw how the stripes reflected the sunlight and created a spectacle of colors. He saw how his black and gray tattoos set him apart from the other elephants and made him unique.

One day, while Rayas was bathing in the river, he saw his reflection in the water. For the first time, he did not see a different elephant, but a beautiful elephant, with stripes that made it unique. He was filled with deep joy and self-love. He understood that to love others, you must first love yourself.

From that day on, Rayas became an ambassador of acceptance. Not only did he convey the message of accepting others for their differences, but they should also love the qualities that made them unique and with which they could do unique things. The savanna became a more tolerant and harmonious place thanks to Rayas' wisdom and love.

Moral: Acceptance begins with yourself. Only when we accept and love ourselves can we love and accept others

Chapter 6
The fight against bullying

The fame of Rayas, the striped elephant, spread across the savannah-like fresh grass in the rainy season. His story of acceptance and respect had inspired many animals but had also made some envious. A group of elephants, led by Bruno, a dark gray pachyderm with a hostile look, constantly made fun of Rayas for being different. They called him "monster" and "freak," and his laughter echoed across the meadow like an echo of cruelty.

One day, while Rayas was walking steadily towards the river, he met the group of elephants that were traveling to the same place, with a slow step on the paved road. Bruno, in his harsh and sarcastic voice, said to him: "What are you doing here, monster? You scare everyone with your strange stripes. You should hide in the jungle where no one sees you."

Bruno's words hurt Rayas' heart, but they did not intimidate him. He stood tall with his majestic presence and, with a calm and firm voice, replied: "I have listened to your taunts for too long. I am not a monster or a freak. I am a different elephant, like many other animals in the world. savanna

The difference" It is not a defect, but an advantage. "They must learn to accept and respect others, regardless of their appearance or characteristics."

And while they were distracted by the exchange of words, no one noticed that a huge truck, driven by a human, was coming in their direction. The elephants moved away from the road, but Bruno, who had the dark gray color of asphalt, was paralyzed with fear. The trucker was about to run over him since he could not distinguish him from the road, but thanks to Rayas who got in the way, the trucker was surprised to see this strange elephant, who turned the steering wheel strongly, avoiding the two elephants.

Faced with such a feat, and understanding that sometimes what is believed to be "normal" is a disadvantage, and on the contrary "what is different" is beneficial, the elephants who were making fun of Rayas reflected. The bullies had shown that they were only strong in appearance and that in reality a "weak" had saved them, and that is why they were filled with shame, lowered their trunks, and apologized.

Rayas, with his wisdom and patience, spoke to the elephants about the importance of tolerance and respect. He told them stories of other animals that were also different and had achieved great things. He taught them that diversity was a source of wealth and that true strength lies in acceptance and togetherness.

From that day on, the arrogant elephants were transformed. They stopped bothering the other animals and became examples of inclusion and harmony in the savanna. Bruno, in particular, became a faithful friend of

Rayas, and together they defended the value of difference in every corner of the forest.

Moral: We cannot tolerate bullying. We must confront those who annoy us for being different and teach them the value of acceptance and respect. Unity and tolerance are the most powerful weapons to build a better world.

Chapter 7

The power of self-esteem

Rayas had come a long way on his journey of self-discovery. She had learned to accept his differences, to love his stripes, and to fight against bullying. However, she was still missing an important step: developing strong self-esteem and defending her values with conviction.

One day, while he was walking in the meadow, he met a wise old tiger. The tiger, with his penetrating gaze, saw the insecurity in Stripes' heart and said to him:

"Stripes, you have achieved a lot, but you still need to believe in yourself. You have incalculable value and you must defend your values firmly. Self-esteem is the basis of success and happiness. You must work on it every day."

The tiger's words resonated in Stripes' heart. He realized that he was right. He couldn't be a leader and an advocate for acceptance if he didn't have confidence in himself.

Rayas began to work on his self-esteem. He repeated positive affirmations to himself every day, focused on his strengths, and faced his fears with courage. As his self-esteem grew, so did his self-confidence and his ability to defend his values.

One day, a group of hunters came to the savanna. The hunters, with their weapons and their cruelty, threatened to destroy the home of Rayas and the other animals. Rayas, without hesitation, stood in front of the pack

and with a firm and confident voice
said to the hunters:

"We will not allow them to destroy our
home. This savanna is our home and
we will defend it with our lives. Respect
nature and the animals that live here."

The hunters, surprised by Rayas' bravery and determination, retreated from the savanna. Rayas became a hero for the pack and a symbol of environmental protection.

Moral: Self-esteem is the basis of success and happiness. We must work on it every day to be able to defend our values with conviction.

Chapter 8

Union make force

The tattooed elephant had incorporated many lessons into his journey of self-discovery. Now, he was ready to put into practice everything he had learned and help others.

One spring evening, the sky roared with lightning and thunder; The rain was pouring down. A little bird, soaked and trembling, watched in despair as his eggs, about to hatch, had become detached from the nest and were now lying on the ground, at the mercy of the storm.

Suddenly, a huge, gentle trunk landed in front of him. It was Rayas, who, upon seeing the little bird's distress, immediately understood the situation.

With his trunk, he carefully lifted the eggs, one by one, and deposited them safely inside his ear. Rayas' soft fur provided them with warmth and protection as the storm subsided.

The little bird, overflowing with gratitude, perched on Stripes's head, chirping happily. Together, they waited for the rain to stop and the sun to shine again.

When the time came, Rayas, with his trunk, lifted the little bird and placed it in a new nest that he had built with branches and dry leaves. The little bird, with its eggs safe and a new house, could not contain his happiness and sang a beautiful song of gratitude.

Rayas, with a smile on his face, walked away, leaving behind a small nest full of hope and a little bird that would never forget his kindness.

When her friends asked her what happened to that little bird, the striped elephant told them what happened and taught the animals the value of

friendship, cooperation, and trust. He showed them that by working together they could achieve great things, even those that seemed impossible. The animals, inspired by Rayas' example, became a strong and united group, capable of facing any challenge.

Moral: Unity is strength. When we work together, we can achieve incredible things.

Chapter 9

The beauty of diversity

One day, while Rayas was drinking from a stream, she encountered a group of animals very different from each other. There was a majestic lion, an elegant giraffe, a mischievous monkey, a wise turtle, and a colorful hummingbird. Rayas, intrigued by the diversity of the group, approached them and began to chat.

Each animal told Stripes about their unique abilities and talents. The lion told him about his strength and leadership, the giraffe about his height and his ability to observe from afar, the monkey about his agility and his sense of humor, the turtle about his wisdom and patience, and the hummingbird about her beauty. and its ability to fly.

Rayas, fascinated by the stories of animals, confirmed what he had always thought, that is, that diversity was a wealth. Each animal, with its unique characteristics, had something special to offer the world. The savanna was a more beautiful and vibrant place thanks to the diversity of its inhabitants. You just have to discover what makes a person unique exploit that benefit, and try to improve where you are weak.

From that day on, Rayas became an advocate for diversity. He taught the other animals that differences were not a reason for division, but for unity. He showed them that everyone, regardless of their appearance or characteristics, had something important to contribute to the world.

Moral: Diversity is a wealth. We all have something special to offer the world.

Chapter 10

A legacy of acceptance

Rayas felt fortunate to lead a life full of learning and transformation. Now, at the end of his life, he was ready to leave a legacy of acceptance for future generations.

He gathered all the animals of the savannah and with his wise and serene voice he told them:

"Dear friends, I have come a long way in my life. I have learned that difference is not a flaw, but a fortune. I have learned that we all have something special to offer the world. I have learned that true strength lies in acceptance, respect, and love.

I want to leave them a legacy of acceptance. I want all of you to learn to accept yourself and others, no matter your appearance, your characteristics, or your beliefs. I want them to live in a world where diversity is celebrated and where everyone feels valued and respected.

Always remember: difference makes us stronger. When we accept and value ourselves, we can build a more beautiful, more harmonious, and more full of possibilities world."

Rayas' words resonated in the hearts of all the animals. They looked at each other with eyes full of hope and understanding. They vowed to continue Rayas' legacy and build a better world for future generations.

Moral: Acceptance is the most valuable legacy we can leave.

End

Other children's literary works by the author that you will find on this platform:

• The challenges of being a mother

• How to become a real-life fairy

• The Wise Giraffe

• The Cat that became a Unicorn

• The Adventures of Rex

-The Tyrannosaurus Astronaut-.

• The Crazy Adventures of the Pirate Parrot

• The Naughty Bear

• The brave dolphin

• Valentin, the aviator monkey

• The elephant with stripes

• Rusky's journey

######O######

EDICIONES
AFRODITA
BELLAS LETRAS